For Parents and Teachers

What's one of the most common ways we make new friends? Through shared interests, right?

New friendships often begin when we find someone who enjoys the same things that we do.

In Daniel Share-Strom's *Do You Want To Play?*, Jamie is so excited to meet a new boy named Dylan who loves to line up his toy cars, because she loves to play with cars more than anything in the world!

When Dylan doesn't respond to her invitation to play, Jamie is confused. When someone tells her that his autism might mean he only wants to play by himself, that makes no sense to her: they both love cars, so why wouldn't he want to play? She just has to try harder.

Jamie doesn't know anything about autism as she tries to have this new boy notice her. She doesn't know that Dylan enjoys playing alone with his cars, and he feels kind of anxious meeting new people. She is simply eager to make a new friend, and asks him, "Do you want to play?"

Dylan may, indeed, want to play, but for him, his autism means an unexpected invitation leaves him unable to respond. It's not that he is ignoring Jamie. He just might not know what to say or do in that moment.

Jamie doesn't give up trying to become friends with Dylan. She shows him lots of new ways to play with his cars and trucks, but he is not happy with Jamie's efforts to get his attention. He really likes to play by lining up his cars, and this girl is just not following the rules!

Will these two *ever* play together?

Do You Want To Play? is a different type of autism-focused book. Unlike the others, it does not insist the Autistic child change who they are to be accepted. Dylan is not portrayed as an object of pity or sympathy, but as an interesting potential friend who sees things a bit differently. The onus is on friendly and determined Jamie not to try to change Dylan, but to view the world from his perspective to foster a relationship.

Jamie doesn't yet know what autism is…she doesn't yet know that some Autistic children respond well to a calm and patient approach, that quietly playing beside the child without any expectations may help to build trust, or the ways in which Autistic people can make their own meaningful contributions to a friendship.

Jamie doesn't know any of those things. She's just a girl who loves cars who wants to make friends with the cool new boy who loves them too.

So, with that in mind…

Do *you* want to play?

Maxine Share, Autism Consultant

Do You WAnt to PLay?

Making Friends with an Autistic Kid

By Daniel Share-Strom RSW
Illustrated by Naghmeh Afshinjah

A NOTE FOR ADULTS

This book uses the term "Autistic" to refer to people with an autism identification, as that is the language most people on the spectrum prefer.

Please refer to our For Parents and Teachers note and Questions & Answers section at the end of the book to enhance your understanding and help guide discussion with your young readers. The latter contains common questions they may have for each page.

Also, please note that Dylan does not represent every Autistic person, as everyone on the autism spectrum is different.

HI, I'M JAMIE!

Today, my friend Caroline was on the swing after school.

I wanted to join her, but someone was on the other swing.

I got bored of waiting my turn and went to play in the sandbox.

Someone new was there...

He was playing with cars.

I love cars!

He wasn't playing like I do, though

Instead of **VROOOM VROOOOOOOMING** them, he was putting them in a loooong line in the sand.

I asked, "**Do you want to play?**"
He didn't answer.
I asked again, "**Do you want to Play?**

He didn't even look at me.

Why?

I didn't understand, so I went back to the swings.

"Caroline, who's that boy?"

"That's Dylan," she said. "My mommy says he's 'Autistic' or 'on the autism spectrum' or something."

"What's autism?"

"I don't know. Maybe it's why he doesn't play with anyone."

...but... he liked cars...

and *I* liked cars...

...so we could be friends, right?

When I went back to the sandbox,
Dylan was still lining up his cars.
I took out my yellow truck.

**"This is my favourite truck!
Do you want to play?"**

Why not?

He didn't even look at it.

Maybe he didn't know any games?
I got sticks and made a highway.

**"We can make a traffic jam!
Do you want to play?"**

But instead of driving on the highway, he moved his cars away.

Maybe his cars needed drivers? I found tiny dollies and put them on Dylan's cars.

"Now they can drive," I said.
"Do you want to play?"

He just frowned,
swiped the dolls off the cars,
and started a second lineup.

Why wouldn't Dylan play cars with me?

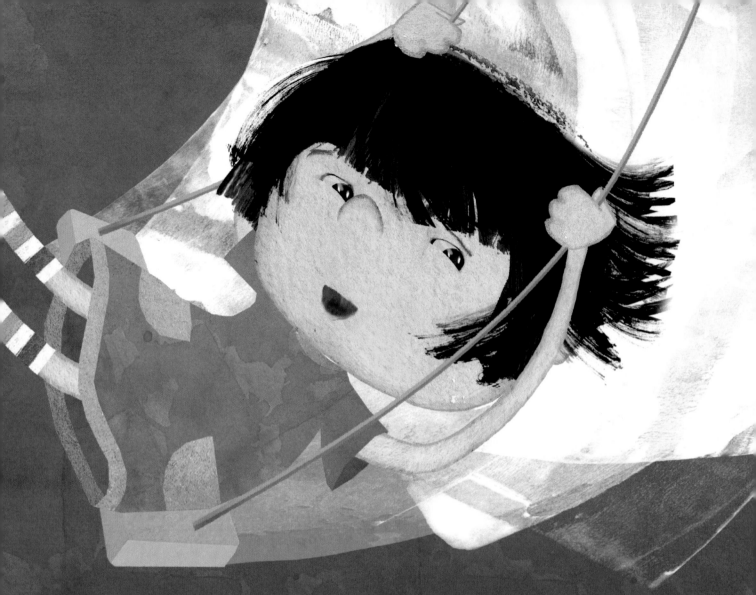

The swing beside Caroline was empty now,
so I went to her.
She asked, "Can you push me?"
I did, and she said, "He didn't play with you, huh?"

"No. I showed him my favourite yellow truck.
I built him a highway. I even gave him drivers.
But he didn't play with me."
"He doesn't play with anyone," said Caroline.

That made me feel a bit sad.

Caroline was swinging high now, so I got on the other one and started to slowly swing.

"You know," Caroline said, "I like when you push me, but swinging beside you is nice, too."

When I got up high, I saw Dylan in the sandbox.

"Yeah. Sometimes it's nice just being beside you..."

We swung quietly.

Wait-that was it!
I jumped off and ran to the sandbox.
"Hey," called Caroline.
"Where are you going?"
Mommy was picking me up soon,
    but I had an idea!

I sat beside Dylan.
He'd almost finished his
second line of cars.
I didn't ask him to play. I just
VROOOOMED my favourite
yellow truck around.
Dylan lined up cars.
That was
okay.

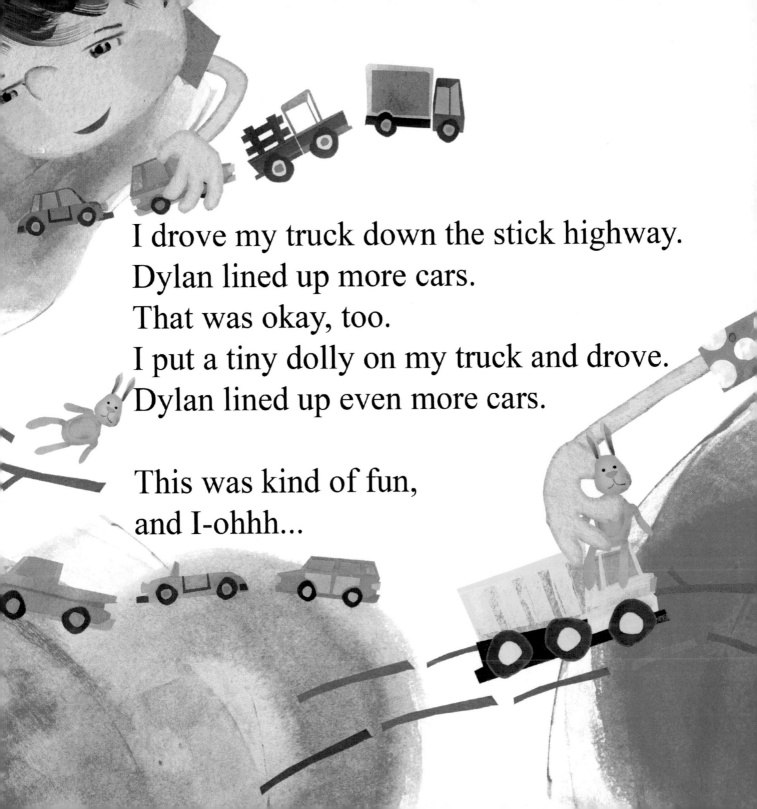

I drove my truck down the stick highway.
Dylan lined up more cars.
That was okay, too.
I put a tiny dolly on my truck and drove.
Dylan lined up even more cars.

This was kind of fun,
and I-ohhh...

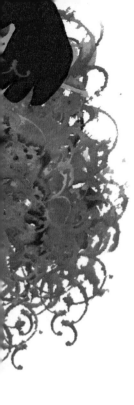

"Jamie!"
Mommy was at the gate.
I ran and hugged her.
She asked, "Sweetie, who's that boy you
were playing with?"

I looked back at the sandbox.
Dylan's cars were there, but he was gone.
"Oh, I couldn't get him to play with me."

As we walked to our big car, I reached in my bag
for my favourite yellow truck.
It wasn't there!
I couldn't see it in the sandbox, either!
I was crying when I felt a tug on my shirt.

Dylan was there, holding something out.

My truck!
Wow, he found it!
"Thanks!"
When I took it, he was looking toward me.

I asked,
"Do... you want to play?"

He said nothing, so Mommy and I
turned to leave.
I felt another tug.
I turned back, and Dylan spoke
to me for the first time.

"Yes."

Do you want to ask some questions?

Pages 6 & 7

Why is the page upside down?

Just like in real life, when you change how you look at things, it can help you understand somebody else's point of view. Turning the book upside down helps you see how Dylan plays.

Why is he lining up cars?

Simple! That's how he likes to play. Some children really like to line up their toys. He sure does. He finds it comfortable and fun to play this way.

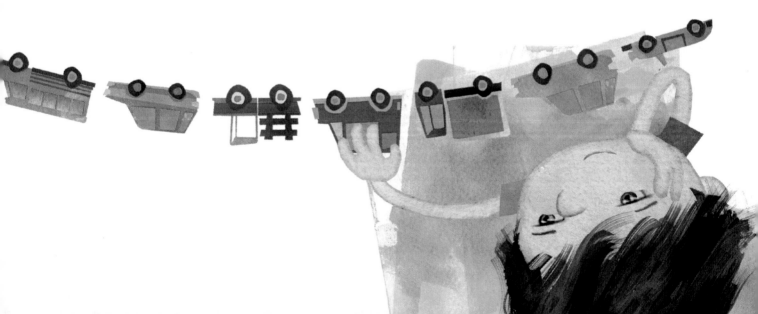

What is autism? What does "Autistic" mean?

Autism is a word that describes how some people interact with others and the world.   Most people with an autism diagnosis like to be called "Autistic," and no two of them are the same.

Some Autistic people speak, while others don't. Some don't like loud noises, but others love to make a racket! Some might be nervous around new people, but others might want to play with everyone! For Dylan, being Autistic means he has trouble speaking and likes to play by lining up his toy cars. Being Autistic is a really cool way of being human.

Can you make friends with someone who is Autistic?

Absolutely! Most Autistic people want friends but might not know how to make them. It helps to be kind, do things they like, and learn about them. An Autistic person might not answer right away when you ask them to play, so be patient, and try again another time. Remember: it's up to them if they want to be friends-no one has to play with people they don't want to.

Why doesn't Dylan play with Jamie? Why does he move his cars away from the stick highway and knock the dollies off his cars?

For Dylan, being Autistic means he might not like new things or sudden changes, and he really loves playing one way: by lining up his red cars. When Jamie tries to get him to play a new way using the stick highway and her yellow truck, or by putting the dollies on his red cars, he doesn't like it. Just like you, Dylan gets frustrated when someone touches his things without permission. Dylan seems frustrated because Jamie is not playing the way he likes to play. He also doesn't know Jamie very well yet, which might make him more uncomfortable. He hasn't learned yet how to use his words to tell her how he feels or what he'd like her to do.

Pages 16 & 17

Why does Jamie walk away from Dylan?

Jamie thinks that Dylan doesn't want to play with her, just like Caroline said. Jamie thinks she has tried everything to get him to play, but nothing has worked. Do *you* think Dylan doesn't want to play with her?

Pages 18 & 19

What does it mean when Jamie says, 'Sometimes it's nice just being beside you…'?

Jamie has realized something important: while it is fun to push Caroline on the swing, she also likes when they both swing quietly beside each other. While it is cool to play by doing things together, she enjoys just being around her friends as well.

Pages 20 & 21

Why does Jamie sit beside Dylan and do everything all over again?

Jamie tries something different this time. She doesn't try to get him to play with her yellow truck, the stuck highway, or the tiny dollies. She plays by herself as he happily lines up his cars. She just hopes he enjoys her company. Do you think he does?

Pages 24 & 25

Why does Dylan tug at Jamie's shirt?

Dylan doesn't talk very much, but he's able to get Jamie's attention by tugging on her shirt. There are lots of ways to communicate with each other besides talking. What do you think he's holding out?

Why does Dylan decide he wants to play with Jamie?

Dylan did not want to play cars the ways Jamie was doing it. He felt uncomfortable with this new girl and her different ways of doing things. However, when she played beside him as he lined up his cars, he felt okay about that. Now, he feels comfortable having her around.

Why has Dylan brought her the yellow truck?

He saw that she left it in the sandbox and thought she would want to have it. Isn't that nice of him?

Why doesn't Dylan look Jamie in the eye?

Some Autistic people look others in the eye and some don't. Those who don't might say it feels embarrassing, or that it is hard to pay attention to anything else when looking into someone's eyes. Either way, it's okay. Autistic people can still hear you and pay attention, even if they are not looking you in the eye.

Why is Dylan holding the yellow truck instead of his cars, and letting her touch his cars now?

After spending some time with Jamie, Dylan feels a bit less anxious and is open to trying something new!

He's pretty cool, huh?

Bios

Daniel Share-Strom, RSW - Author

Daniel Share-Strom is a Registered Social Worker raised in York Region, Ontario. He's been a motivational speaker and workshop facilitator for 15 years, telling stories of his own experiences growing up Autistic and advising families and professionals how to help their loved ones, clients, and students on the autism spectrum to live their best possible lives. Together with his mother, Maxine Share, he co-founded social initiative Autism Goggles, so named because it helps people to see the world through an autism lens.

He has completed Honours programs in Social Work and Communication, as well as a post-grad certificate in Children's Media and a certificate in Positive Psychology. It is Daniel's belief that we can change the world with the messaging we provide to our children. Daniel lives in Bradford, Ontario, with two parents and far too many dogs and cats. *Do You Want to Play?* is his first children's book, but it won't be his last!

Naghmeh Afshinjah – Illustrator

Born in Tehran, Iran, Naghmeh Afshinjah has been a visual artist her entire life. A self-taught painter in different media with a Bachelor's Degree in Graphic Design, she has worked as a graphic designer, art director, and illustrator for over 25 years.

After many years in these roles and several more dedicated to focusing on her loving Autistic son, Naghmeh opened up a home art studio. She currently teaches watercolour classes and workshops to adults and children in Stouffville, Ontario.

Maxine Share - Autism Consultant

Maxine Share is an Autistic writer, autism consultant, workshop developer, and facilitator who is a passionate champion of the strengths and potential of Autistic people across the spectrum of abilities. With her son Daniel, she created the popular full-day workshop called 'What Doctors Don't Tell You and Teachers Don't Know' to provide critical information to parents, educators, and other helping professionals who want to help Autistic students to thrive. She is a member of the Ontario government's Minister's Advisory Committee on Special Education.

She and Daniel run the Facebook group Autism Goggles, where her articles move readers to an informed understanding of what it can mean to be Autistic. Maxine's mission in life is to change understanding of autism to change the actions of others. She believes that when society understands that autism is just another way of being human, her work will be done. Maxine consulted on *Do You Want to Play?*.

Acknowledgements

Wow—I've written academic papers dozens of pages long, and this 'simple' children's book is the hardest thing I've written in my life. *Do You Want to Play?* was written not with a keyboard and monitor, but with my heart and my soul.

It wouldn't have been possible without a cadre of amazing people. With that I mind, I'd like to acknowledge:

- My amazing mother, Maxine Share, who consulted to make sure Jamie and Dylan's experiences were accurate and presented appropriately, who instilled strong values in me, and who convinced me to write a book in the first place. I love you and admire your strength, tenacity, and courage in advocating for a better world for autistic people.

- My dear friend and colleague Flora Doohan, who stood beside me through the entire writing process, keeping me on-track and serving as the proverbial wall for me to bounce ideas off, even when I was pacing up and down the halls of Centennial College, ripping my hair out as I tried to find out how to use swings to have Jamie come to her ultimate revelation about how to play with Dylan. Thank you for keeping me sane.

- My former Children's Media program coordinator, Liz Haines, who oversaw the writing process and, on seeing the final product, immediately volunteered her services and contact list to help get the property out there in the media world. I owe you big time.

- My Children's Books teacher, Erin Thomas, for providing editing services and crucial guidance on the format and language of children's books. This would never have worked without your assistance.

- My phenomenally talented illustrator, Naghmeh Afshinjah, who brought Jamie, Dylan, and the other characters to life in a way that made me do a double-take when I first saw it. She immediately captured the vision I had of a whimsical, emotionally powerful story, and her experience in the autism world allowed her to capture a level of fine detail that might otherwise have been impossible. Thanks for bringing that tear to my eye.

Daniel Share-Strom

Made in the USA
Middletown, DE
08 November 2022

14436674R00022